MW00913786

Bible Camp Bloodbath

JOEY COMEAU

First edition November 2010
Copyright © Joey Comeau, 2010

This is a work of fiction. I think. Names, characters, and places are the product of the author's imagination, or are used fictitiously, and any resemblance to actual persons, living or dead, is probably cause for alarm.

Printed in the USA

ISBN 145387769X
EAN-13 9781453877692

Cover by Joey Comeau
Design by Emily Horne
Drawing by Kate Beaton
Edited by Derek McCormack
Tony's wardrobe by Maison Martin Margiela

This book is set in Baskerville.

for
DEREK MCCORMACK

1.

"I got the job!" Martin's mother announced. She tossed her bag on the pile of shoes by the front door and came into the living room, scooping Martin up in her arms. "I'm going to be spending three weeks making flaps of wet torn skin, jutting white broken bones, and drooling chunks of flesh for *Blood Socket 2*. *Blood Socket 2*, Martin! Pus! Spleens! Teeth! I'll be spreading fake guts all over the walls. They said they loved my work in particular on *Undead Hungry Grandmother Birthday Party*. I didn't think anyone even saw that movie."

Martin squeezed his mother while she spun him around the room. He kissed her neck. She was so happy. This would be good for them. She was always happiest when she was working on the movies. She was too good for the makeup counter at the mall. She was too smart.

"You may have to go and stay with your aunt and uncle for a few weeks," she said. "A lot of the filming is going to be in Toronto, so I'll have to stay in a hotel. Those filthy big city streets will run with blood. They'll have to install blood gutters."

For dinner they had an ice cream cake. Vanilla with a chocolate crumble centre, and on the top of it, in pink glossy icing, it read, "Happy Birthday Lucifer, Our Sugary Dark Lord." A celebration! Tonight she would have her friends over and Martin would be sent to bed while they partied late, but right now it was just the two of them. They sat at the kitchen table eating ice cream cake while Martin's mother sketched ideas for gore effects. Martin rested his head on her shoulder and together they planned the perfect dangling kitten eyeballs.

* * *

Martin had a picture he'd clipped from a magazine of a goat standing on the back of a cow. It seemed otherworldly to him, but neither the goat nor the cow looked concerned. They didn't care that the goats in picture books never stood on cows. They pulled this shit all the time. This was just how it was. His mother had that same look on her face, up on the kitchen table with someone else's bottle of wine in her hand, head tilted to avoid the light fixture. Martin could see mud caked around the edges of her boots, smeared on the tabletop.

He stayed quiet, out of sight. He knew how this worked. It was against the rules for her to wear her boots in the house, but if he spoke up the response would be, "Bed time, kiddo." Forget that. He liked to watch his mother when she was around her friends. As long as the table didn't break again, it was okay. Mud was easy to clean up.

* * *

With his baggy shirts and wire rim glasses, Martin looked like he'd been picked too soon. He was eleven years old, and he wore button-up shirts that were always too big on him. He looked like the kind of kid who cut pictures of goats standing on cows out of magazines, like the kind of kid who was proud

8

when people called him a nerd. And he was proud. His mother was a nerd. Sure she was a violent and unpredictable nerd who dressed like a panhandling teen, but she was a nerd. She knew more about chemistry than any of his teachers. Sometimes, just for fun, she made the strangest things broil and ooze for Martin. For his last birthday, she set a Halloween mask over a shot glass full of mystery sludge, so that sickly foam drooled and spat from the mouth. Martin made her repeat the trick again and again, watching the foaming grin in horror.

* * *

Up on the table, Martin's mother cleared her throat to quiet the room. When that didn't work, she stomped her boot. Everyone turned to look, and she gave a small curtsy. She took a drink from the bottle of wine, an empty glass in her other hand, then she raised both over the whole room.

"To the Royal goddamned Bank of Canada, and their kindhearted vat-grown employees," she said, "for being so understanding of the plight of a young single mother. God bless their tiny little hearts and may none of them be out sick or on vacation when I go down there to burn their building to the ground."

Everyone laughed. His mother wore the white t-shirt with the sleeves torn off. Across the front there was a black drawing of a crow. It clung to a branch that ran around to her back, out of sight. It was one of her favourite t-shirts. The tail end of her snake tattoo came winding down the skin of her arm from her shoulder.

"No wait!" she said. "This is a celebration. Fuck the banks. I got the job! I am gonna help make people feel sick to their stomachs! I'm contributing to society! Little kids hiding behind couches, that will be my legacy! Turn the music up!" his mother yelled. "Turn it up!" She stomped her boot on the table. "Let's see how those shit dicks downstairs like it for once."

Everyone sang and laughed at the same time, and some-one turned the music up. Martin's mother took another drink. She stomped again. She stomped her boot one more time, and the table broke under her weight. Crack.

Martin's heart closed for that half second while his moth-er's eyes were white and her arms were thrown up in the air. He lost track of the wine. He lost track of her friends. All Martin could see was the startled look on her face.

She landed on the broken table and slid to the side, roll-ing when she hit the floor. Martin held his breath. There was a crunch. Martin's mother was okay. That crunch was just the wine glass. She sat stunned on the floor. Then she smiled and came alive.

"Fucking bullshit." She scrambled to wipe up the red wine with the bottom of her shirt and with the tablecloth. "Fuck-ing dog garbage," she said. She was ruining her shirt and the tablecloth and laughing. She wasn't hurt. Martin couldn't help it, he laughed too. This was a cheap table they bought at a yard sale to replace the last one. Next time they were going to have to buy something that could support her weight.

"Dog garbage" was something she said all the time. Mar-tin had started saying it, too. Not on purpose, but he caught him-self saying it every once in a while. When people spend all their time together, they start to talk the same.

* * *

"Your shirt is filthy," Tom, the skinny one, said to Mar-tin's mother. "I advise you to take it off immediately." Laughter. And then, after a second, Tom said, "That's what I'm talking about!"

Martin couldn't see what was going on. He tore a square of the paper towel off the roll and carefully folded it twice into perfect quarters. He tore another square off and folded it twice. This would be good to start. Then he could come back for more.

If he took too long, the wine would have longer to stain. He elbowed through the group of them all crowded around his mother. She was in her bra now, shirt in hand. The room got quiet when Martin pushed through to give her the paper towel.

"Oh, great," Tom said, "there goes our fun." Martin could feel them looking at him, but he didn't care. If she didn't get that shirt dealt with, it would stain. The wine would stain the floor, too. It always had to be red wine. "Kid, fuck off," Tom said. Martin ignored him, and crouched beside his mother. He offered the folded paper towels.

"It's red wine," Martin said. It was a stupid thing to say. She knew it was red wine.

2.

Martin woke in the dark, certain that there was a man in the bedroom with him. He covered his mouth to keep from making any noise and listened. There were quiet sounds from the street coming through the window, but what else? Was there someone breathing? A man could be standing there above him, just smiling. Any second he could whisper Martin's name, his lips pulling back slowly, his hairy fingers slick with sweat. Martin was going to scream and kick and thrash. He could feel it. He closed his eyes and pulled the comforter tighter. Nobody was there. It was just the dream again. Nobody was there. He held the blanket tight to protect himself, and eventually he fell back asleep.

* * *

In the morning he woke up from a much nicer dream. He was planting bushes in his grandmother's garden, and one of the bushes was actually a lost kitten. The sun was so bright it was almost invisible in the sky. Sometimes you just know things in a dream. Martin dug a small hole in the dirt and planted a dark green bush with wide leaves that was also a lost kitten. It meowed. Meow. Meow. Meow. And then Martin was awake and that repeating sound was his mother's alarm in the other room. The window was open and it was cool in his room. The alarm kept going. All his blankets were on the floor.

Martin stood up before he was really awake and stood there for a second. He picked his glasses up off the dresser and dressed for the day. His clothes from last night still needed to be folded and put away. The alarm kept going and for a second he was torn. Should he deal with his mother or fold his clothes? His clothes were just crumpled on the floor. They had to be folded. So he folded fast, but carefully, tucked the clothes into the dirty laundry hamper and then hurried down the hall to the kitchen.

The table knelt broken in the broken glass. The wooden legs jutted out from underneath it in crazy directions so that the table looked like a baby horse trying to stand up for the first time. Someone - probably one of his mother's friends - had tried to clean up the glass. They'd swept some of it into a pile against the kitchen wall. A half-assed job. There were still shards everywhere. Martin took the broom and cleared a path to the counter and the fridge, so it was safe to walk in his socks.

He made his mother tea. No cream. No sugar. The cup rattled on the saucer as he carried it to her room. The more he tried to hold still, the more it rattled.

His mom was sprawled asleep on the bed, facedown in the pillow, and Martin turned the alarm off and set her tea on the nightstand. She had a much darker room than he did and the shades were always drawn in the mornings. It took him a second to adjust to the dim light. There were shelves and shelves of books against the wall and books stacked on the floor beside them. Martin looked around for anything he could clean up before he woke her. Her clothes were strewn and there was a pile of her special effects books on the end of the bed, by her ankles. Martin folded her clothes and placed them in the hamper. He

14

stacked the books on her dresser beside a broken tube of lipstick.

On the dresser mirror, in thick red lipstick, his mother had written, "Get your fucking shit together!" and when he first saw it, Martin thought it was directed at him. But it wasn't. It never was. He sat down on the edge of the bed beside her. The snake tattoo curled all over the skin on her back, jet black with twists of green. The eyes were looking right at him.

"Hello," he whispered to it, and the snake twisted a little as Martin's mother shifted in her sleep. He kissed the tips of his fingers and reached out and touched them to the snake's nose. "Hello, good morning," Martin whispered. The snake's name was Sicily, like the place. When Martin touched his fingers to Sicily, he could hear the snake slithering, like a slow rasp.

He liked this part of the day, just sitting with Sicily in the morning, before his mother woke up. It was calm. The sun was out there, but it couldn't get into the room until they let it. The world hadn't started yet.

Martin poked his mother in the back and she groaned and rolled over a bit, but she didn't wake up. So he shook her shoulder, careful where to grip, not squeezing Sicily. His mother grunted. She opened her eyes and stared at Martin for a second before she realized what was happening.

Martin looked down at his hands while she wrapped herself in a blanket. Part of Sicily's tail went around the front of his mother's body, where you weren't supposed to look. Martin picked up her tea from the dresser and held it out.

"Thanks," she said. It took her a minute to wake up and for a while she just sat on the edge of her bed sipping the tea. She didn't smile and say, "Was I a total idiot last night or what?" the way she always did. Instead, she stared at the words on the mirror and she drank her tea quietly. After she was done, she sat for a few minutes more, wrapped in her bed sheet. Sicily's tail peeked out at Martin and he smiled at it. "I'm sorry," his mother said after a while. Martin shrugged his shoulders, even though he didn't know what she was sorry for. "I'm sorry you had to see

15

me like that last night." Did she mean in her bra? She was naked right now. It didn't matter to Martin.

"Whatever," he said. "It's okay. Nothing I haven't seen before!" He laughed, and he expected her to laugh too. "Nothing I haven't seen before" was what she always said when he was having a bath and she had to pee. She'd say, "Nothing I haven't seen before," and then it was okay for her to come in.

It wasn't the right thing to say now, though. She set the teacup down and started crying. Martin didn't know what else to do so he hugged her. He wrapped his arms around her and pushed his head into her shoulder and squeezed hard.

"I love you," Martin said. "And you can't be sad. Did you forget about *Blood Socket 2*?" She unwrapped herself from his arms and kissed his cheek.

"How could I forget about *Blood Socket 2*?" she said. Then she saw what time it was. "Fuck Jesus, I'm late."

2.

Martin slammed the door to the classroom behind himself. It echoed down the hallway in a really satisfying way. He stood in the hallway squeezing both fists as hard as he could until the muscles in his fingers ached. His eyes were filling up with tears, he was so angry. He kicked the wood of the door. He kicked it again, hard. Inside the classroom, everyone would be laughing or staring at the door. He kicked it again.

Hands grabbed him from behind, and Martin twisted and lashed out with his feet, kicking and thrashing. He kicked and kicked until the hands let him go.

"Jesus Christ," the vice-principal said. "Are you done?" Martin tried to keep from crying. When he got angry, his eyes watered, but he wasn't crying. He should count to ten. Those were the rules. Count to ten when you're angry. If you're still angry, count again. Martin was angry. He wasn't crying. "Oh, now you're going to give me the waterworks?" the vice-principal said.

Martin squeezed his fists as hard as he could. "I'm not crying," he said.

"I suppose you weren't just kicking that door, either," the vice-principal said. "What's all this? Why are you out here? What did that door ever do to you?"

"I got kicked out," Martin said. The door opened, and his teacher stepped into the hallway, pulling the door closed. She was younger than Martin's mother, but not as pretty. She wore her hair in a pony tail.

"This is what he handed in for today's quiz," she said. She was smiling at the vice-principal. In the classroom she had been furious, but here she was smiling. Martin couldn't tell which one was real. She showed the vice-principal Martin's quiz sheet, on which he had drawn his teacher, with her eyeball popping out of her head. He had spent a lot of time drawing that eyeball. He didn't know the answers to the quiz questions, but he had still wanted to impress the teacher. He liked her. "I don't think that's very respectful, do you?" she said. She was smiling, but ignoring Martin completely.

"It's not a very good likeness, either," The vice-principal was smiling now, too. "I'll take him down to the office."

"Thanks, Carl."

* * *

"Does your mother know you're calling?" Martin's grandmother said. In the background he could hear his grandfather asking for the phone, but she covered the phone and said, "Go put your teeth in, for goodness' sake. You look like a chicken without a beak."

"I wanted to ask you," Martin said.

"Your mother was very clear with us about how she feels, Martin. She doesn't want anything to do with the church." Martin knew that his mother was an atheist. He knew it the way he knew she was twenty-nine years old. It was just a fact. It didn't seem important to who she was.

"I just think Bible Camp sounds fun," he said. "And I know that we can't afford it, but I remember last year you said that the church would pay for me. And I don't think she'll mind. This way I'm not a burden on anyone."

"Of course they'll pay," Martin's grandmother said. "They send a dozen kids every year, I'm sure they'd be happy to help you, too. But you shouldn't be asking behind your mother's back." In the background, Martin's grandfather said something else.

"What did he say?" Martin asked.

"Oh, don't mind him," she said. "Now he looks like a chicken with its teeth in."

* * *

"If this is what you want," Martin's mother said. "Then I'll call your uncle and tell him that you won't be staying at their place."

"You're not mad?" Martin said.

"Why would I be mad?" she said. "I went to that camp when I was a kid. It was fun enough. It wasn't for me, but that's a choice I made myself. You have to figure it out on your own, I guess."

"You mean about whether I believe in God?" Martin said and his mother laughed.

"I don't mean to laugh, honey," she said. "No, Martin. Not about whether you believe in God or not. I mean whether you enjoy sitting around a campfire every night, getting eaten alive by mosquitoes, singing pop songs with all the words changed so they are about Jesus."

"Oh," Martin said. "One more question?"

"Out with it."

"You'll save me some eyeballs?" Martin said.

"Of course," she said. "I'll mail you a big tub of eyeballs at camp, return address marked: "The bowels of Hell." That'll help you make friends, I'm sure. And Martin?" She knelt so their faces were at the same level. "I might even send you some blood-stained teeth."

* * *

On the last day of school, Zoe and Christine gave Martin a small box of chocolates wrapped in a bow. There was a small folded card and they smiled and watched him open it.

"We voted you best fixer-upper," Zoe said. She had her baseball cap on backward today and her jeans were torn and dirty as always. The other girls were all over by the picnic table, but Zoe and Chris had come to meet Martin halfway. "You don't have to give a speech or anything," Zoe said.

"Thank you," Martin said. He couldn't tell if it was a joke or not. He was never really sure with Zoe and her friends. Sometimes he got the feeling that they thought of him like an alien life form or an animal in a zoo. But mostly he felt like one of the crowd. He liked to be around them. They talked and laughed and hatched plots and he could just sit and listen. He could just be carried along without worrying about anything. And they seemed to like him, too. They liked that he occasionally went nuts and drew teachers with their eyeballs popping out. But more than that, they liked that he sat and listened.

"We're going to egg Fowler's car," Chris said. "Zoe's going to the store while everyone is at the assembly so you need to give her a dollar if you want your own egg."

"I do!" Martin said. He found a dollar in his pocket and gave it to Zoe. Then he opened his chocolates and smiled. "Thank you for the chocolates," he said.

"We're gonna miss you this summer," Chris said. "Bible Camp! That sounds terrible."

"Tell Jesus we said hi," Zoe said.

4.

The driveway to the Bible Camp was long and narrow. It wasn't wide enough for two cars, though it was clearly meant to be both entrance and exit. It went past a small billboard with the camp's name and down between two large fields. Badminton nets across the field on the left, and a line of archery targets on the right. The driveway continued on down into the trees.

Martin held his mother's hand as they drove. The trees were so close that the branches closed above them, so that, after the brilliant sunlight, it felt as though they were driving into darkness. The path twisted and turned and Martin had no idea what they would do if they came across another car.

And then the trees to their right pulled back to reveal a small white chapel with a stained glass window above the front door and with a cluster of headstones beside it. Martin twisted in his seat as they passed, trying to see the headstones more clearly. Were they new or old? But then they were back in the trees and the shadow.

The camp was bright and open, though. There were a half-dozen cars parked in front of the big main building. Children and parents were standing around and smiling. The main building was white, too, like a farmhouse kind of white, all cracked paint and wooden siding. There were screens on the doors and windows.

"Last chance to change your mind," Martin's mother said.

* * *

Tony, the head counsellor, approached the microphone and tapped it a few times until everyone stopped talking. His uniform was dark brown and he looked friendly. Martin sat lower in his seat. This was going to be a long two weeks, but it was better than staying with his uncle. Tony tapped the microphone again. There were posters up on the wall here, inspirational things about Jesus and about the Holy Father and the Bible. "Have you read this year's real best seller?" Things like that.

"First let me tell you a little bit about why we run this camp every year," Tony said. "Every year we hike out here to the woods and we live in these little cabins with all you rowdy kids for one reason and one reason only. Because it's fun. Running this camp for the past two years, I don't think I've ever had more fun. We have swimming and archery and orienteering and arts and crafts and we have capture the flag and we have a bonfire every week where we sing and play guitar and I don't know one camper who hasn't had the time of his life." He caught himself. "His or her life.

"Last year we had a girl who got stung by six jellyfish when she was out swimming. She was stung pretty badly and we had to call her parents and arrange to take her to the hospital. When she was getting into the car, she wouldn't stop crying, and I told her that she was going to be okay. She was going to be fine. And do you know what she said to me? She said, 'I'm not going to be fine, I'm going to miss the bonfire tonight!'" He laughed.

"Here I was, trying to console her because she had been stung so badly, and that wasn't why she was upset at all! She just wanted to stay and have more fun!"

The other counsellors all laughed along with Tony. The campers did, too. Martin made himself laugh, no louder than anyone else, but no quieter, either. There was a girl with a single feather earring sitting two rows ahead. She wasn't laughing. She leaned over to one of her friends and whispered something. Martin should have sat closer to them. They seemed more interesting than anyone else here.

"But I'll stop talking about how fun it is, and I'll let you go and figure it out for yourself," Tony said. "Just let me ask one question and when you've answered it, just get up and head into the next room where we've got cake and juice and milk and plenty of other stuff they probably didn't tell me about because they were afraid I'd eat it all before you got here!"

The counsellors and campers all laughed again.

"Have you accepted Jesus into your heart?" Tony was serious now. "That sounds like a simple question and maybe it is, but have you accepted Jesus into your heart? Don't answer right away. Give it a minute. Look inside your heart and when you find Jesus there, just stand quietly and head into the next room. If you can't find him, I just want to sit down and talk with you for a few minutes. Nobody's in trouble, here, so let's be honest."

Two rows ahead, the girl and her two friends jumped to their feet and headed to the next room. There was no hesitation, no soul searching, no deep reflection on what it meant to accept Jesus into your heart. Martin followed them.

* * *

Tony came down from the podium and smiled at his counsellors. They were all wearing their uniforms, except for Angela. Angela was wearing jeans and a camp t-shirt. There was no reason not to wear the uniforms. It wasn't more difficult to put on uniform pants instead of jeans. And uniforms served a functional purpose, instilling trust in the campers and providing a clear visual marker of authority. It wasn't going to spoil Tony's day, though. Look at all those campers, smiling and fresh faced. Plump and ready for a summer of fun!

"How'd I do?" Tony said. He knew how he did, though. He gave the same speech every year. "They seemed to like it."

"Good," Chip said, "That was smart, going with the jellyfish story instead of mentioning the kid who got his hand cut off. Good call." He laughed, and a couple of the other counsellors laughed with him. Chip had blonde streaks in his hair. Were those called highlights? Tony didn't know for sure.

Tony sighed.

"Try to be respectful, Chip," he said.

* * *

The girl with the single earring was named Melissa. Her friends were Courtney and Joan. Martin sat down at the table with them and listened as a counsellor introduced herself. The counsellor was wearing an all brown uniform, too. Her name was Cindy, she said.

"So what do you girls like to do for fun?" Cindy said. "There's no TV or internet out here, but we've got girls' softball and soccer!"

"You name the sport, we love it," Courtney said. "Soccer, football, rugby!"

"Rugby!" Cindy laughed. "Well, that's a bit intense for me. I'm more of a volleyball girl."

"Oh we're sports nuts," Courtney said. "We love intense! Intense is right up our alley."

"I like volleyball," Melissa said. Cindy smiled, and adjusted her counsellor uniform.

"What about you?" Cindy said to Joan. Joan just looked down at her hands.

24

"She likes volleyball, too," Melissa said.

"This is going to be fun. I'm glad I got you girls, this year. Some years I get stuck with real weirdos, you know? And before lights out tonight, we'll turn that room upside down until we find your other earring, Melissa."

"And you can tell us everything you know about that counsellor Chip!" Courtney said. "We saw you talking to him!"

"Well, I don't know if it'd be right to tell you girls everything," Cindy laughed and then she was off, introducing herself to another table.

"God, I thought she was going to bother us all night," Courtney said.

"Tell us everything you know!" Melissa said, holding her hands together up by her head and batting her eyelashes. "Oh, he's so dreamy." She made a horking sound. "What did she mean about my other earring?"

"What do you mean, what did she mean?" Courtney said. "You're only wearing one."

"So? I only have one."

"Well, usually people wear two earrings, one in each ear, Melissa."

"Are you taking her side now? Maybe tonight you can curl up in bed beside her, talking about boys while Joan and I go watch for the comet alone. You don't mind if I borrow your telescope?"

"You wouldn't know what to do with it," Courtney said. "You'd just get all confused by a piece of equipment that powerful. You're better off staying with that kid's toy of yours." Melissa wasn't listening. She was looking at Martin. Courtney just kept talking. "It's always something, isn't it? In the city there's too much ambient light to get a clear look at the sky. And out here in the woods there are idiots. I guess there are idiots in the city, too, but we don't have to share a cabin with them." Then she noticed Martin, too. She stopped talking, and the three girls sat staring, waiting for Martin to say something. He didn't.

"What's your name?" Melissa said.

"Martin."

"Well, Martin, can we help you? Is there some reason you're eavesdropping on our conversation?"

Martin thought about it for a second before answering. "Will you show me your telescope?" he said.

5.

Martin was assigned to Cabin Seven. Chip showed him the way.

"You're going to be in one of the old cabins," Chip said. "The girls all live in the new cabins." He pointed to the ridge that overlooked the ocean. The cabins didn't look like cabins at all. They looked like regular buildings, all made out of cement, bright lights inside.

"Air conditioning, plumbing, the works," Chip said, still pointing to the girl cabins. "We just built them this year. There are plans to build more after the season's over, but for now the boys have got the same cabins as always." He winked at Martin and said, "That's what camp is all about, if you ask me. Haunted cabins and having to run through the woods in the middle of the night to pee."

Martin could see the old cabins now, wooden and broken-down looking, set back in the woods. They blended in with the trees around them.

"You aren't afraid of ghosts, are you?" Chip said, winking again. People look so stupid when they wink.

There was a boy in the cabin already. Brown hair. Skinny. Weird teeth.

"Hey," he said, sticking his hand out for Martin. "I'm Ricky."

"My name's Martin," Martin said. The two boys shook hands and Chip grinned.

"You can have any bunk you want," Ricky said. "Except this one's Adrian's, and that one in the corner on the bottom is mine. You should take that other corner bunk so I don't have to sleep near a weirdo. You get some weirdo kids at summer camp," he said. "They let anyone in." Chip laughed at that.

Martin walked to the other corner bunk and set his suitcase on the bed.

"Already settled right in," Chip said. "Look at him. He's not afraid to live in the haunted cabin."

There was nowhere for Martin to unpack his clothes. His shirts were going to have to stay folded in the suitcase, which was unacceptable. There were no closets here, no drawers. Nowhere to hang a hanger. The glass in the window was broken. Martin took a deep breath and let it go. This was where he was now. In a cabin, in the woods.

There weren't supposed to be drawers in a cabin. The windows were meant to be broken and ragged. Get in the spirit, Martin told himself. Think of it like a horror movie. A haunted cabin, like Chip said. Don't worry about your clothes. Worry about who's going to die first. Who will find the body? Will it have all its limbs? Think about an axe cutting through the air. This was an adventure.

His shirts were going to get creases.

* * *

Outside, Ricky showed Martin the Flying Fox. It was a wire tied to two poles. One of the poles was short so the wire was just above their heads, and the other pole was five feet higher and twenty feet away.

You climbed up a ladder to the higher pole and took hold of this metal bar. Then you jumped and held on like your life depended on it and you went flying along the wire toward the shorter pole. At Martin's school they just called this a zip line. Here it was the Flying Fox.

"There was a kid, like, five years ago," Ricky said, "who didn't let go in time, and he bounced right off that short pole and landed on his head. Everyone could hear his neck snap. I know a kid who was here that year and he said he was over by the canteen and he still heard the kid's neck snap. Everyone watching heard the weird grinding sound when the kid tried to get up again. Every single person said they couldn't forget that sound even if they wanted to."

You could tell Ricky had told the story before. He made little hand gestures the whole time. Every time he said "snap" he pretended to break a stick with his hands. Snap. Snap. After he said "grinding" he made a sound in his throat that was not right.

"I'll be back in a couple minutes," Chip said. "I have to go collect our other campers" He waved and headed back toward the main building, leaving Martin alone with Ricky.

"He didn't die, either," Ricky said. "That's the sick part. He's still alive out west somewhere. Somewhere where there's no hills, because he pushes around a wheelchair that he controls with his tongue. I heard that every once in a while his head comes loose, and it rolls around on his neck because the bones aren't connected. Someone has to come and help him put it back in his plastic brace. Otherwise it just swings down and he has to look at his chest all day."

Another pair of boys was coming toward the cabin. The kid on the right had long hair down to his shoulders and he had the bluest eyes Martin had ever seen. The kid on the left was fat and he was wearing all black even though it was hot out. Ricky saw where Martin was looking and he nodded.

"What did I tell you?" he said. "Dressing all in black on a day like this. Man. Weirdo kids."

* * *

Martin woke in the dark, terrified that there was a man in the room with him. It was too dark. The blankets felt wrong. It took him a minute to remember he was at camp. It was darker here than his room at home. He breathed in and out and counted to ten as quietly as he could. He felt certain that there was a man in the dark there, about to whisper his name. Already smiling. Martin counted to ten again and then backwards from ten. He wasn't going to scream. He could control himself. He pulled the blanket tighter and listened.

Nothing. There was nothing. Nobody there in the dark.

Would Ricky be able to help him if something happened? Or Chip? Chip was right in the next room. Would Chip be able to help? But what could they do? Nobody would help him. He was certain. He might as well be alone. Martin squeezed his eyes closed and it didn't make any difference. The dark was there, too. And in the dark, the man. He tried to breathe in and out calmly. When he was almost asleep again, he thought he heard a man's voice whisper a name, but it wasn't his name, and it didn't wake him up.

6.

Franklin stood at bat, his hands gripping the wooden baseball bat tightly. Twisting on the tape wrapped around the handle. The pitcher pitched and the ball went right past. Again. All day the ball had been speeding right past. How many times was he going to have to stand here? Behind Franklin, Jim was the catcher, twelve years old with a high pitched voice.

"Strike two!" Jim yelled.

A trickle of sweat came down from Franklin's brow. He gripped the bat tighter and waited for the next pitch. The pitcher lifted his foot, tilted back and threw the ball and Franklin swung hard. He swung hard, the bat missing the ball entirely and whipping back toward the catcher. It hit Jim's leg below the knee with a crack. The bone snapped, cutting out through the skin of the leg.

Jim screamed.

The coach was there in a second, kneeling down beside Jim while Franklin dropped the bat and backed away.

"It was an accident," Franklin said.

"Don't look," the coach said. The shard of bone stuck up through Jim's skin. Jim cried and looked away. "It doesn't look bad," the coach said. He lifted the leg a little and lowered his face so that he could see better. There was blood pouring out from around the shard of bone now, dark and thick. "In fact," he said, "it looks good." With that the coach gripped the leg tight and ran his tongue along the white bone, licking up the blood, sucking on the marrow.

"What the hell," a man yelled from behind him. "Goddamnit, turn so that the camera can see what you're doing. And can we get some more blood on that bone? It looks like a candy cigarette." The coach stood up and went over to talk to the director. Martin's mother came over and knelt down next to Jim, holding the tube of darker blood.

"You're doing good," she said to Jim, but the kid just shrugged his shoulders.

"It's just a horror movie," the kid said. "I can do better. I'm going to do better. My mom has another audition lined up for me next week." He sounded defensive. Martin's mother just tried to focus on applying the blood. What kind of messed up priorities did this kids' parents give him, where he felt bad about being in a horror movie?

A black cat came over and nuzzled against Jim's leg, mewing softly. It looked up at Martin's mother and then its eyeball popped out with a sick wet sound, splattering her face with blood. The eyeball hung from the socket by a thin thread of purple red veins and muscle. The cat let out a terrified yowl and took off running.

It had taken hours to set up that eyeball effect and now she would have to do it again.

* * *

Mitchell Hemsworth sat on the edge of the washing machine. He had blonde hair and blue, blue eyes and right now

32

they were rimmed in red. He wanted to accept Jesus into his heart. He did. But he didn't know what that felt like. He felt normal. He didn't feel filled with light or saved.

"No, it's not like that," Tony, the head counsellor said. "You let Jesus into your heart by having faith in him. Those other feelings, they come over time. It's not like flicking a switch, son. Nothing in this life is as easy as that."

Mitchell wiped his nose on the back of his hand and looked out the window where the other campers were running around and shrieking with laughter. He had followed the crowd yesterday when everyone went into the other room for cake. Tony had stood up and asked them if they'd accepted Jesus into their hearts and Mitchell hadn't known. He wanted to let Jesus into his heart. But everyone else went into the next room like they were sure and Mitchell followed.

And then this morning his counsellor had found Mitchell crying in bed, with the Bible under his pillow, and he'd taken him down to see Tony. Mitchell had worries. If he did accept Jesus into his heart, he would be saved, he would live forever in Heaven, but would his dad? His dad was an atheist and Tony had said that there was nothing Mitchell could do to save his dad from Hell.

"But it won't bother you," Tony said. He put his hand on the boy's head and tousled his hair. "You'll be in a better place. You won't even notice that your dad isn't with you." Tony smiled. "Here, I have something for you." He reached up behind Mitchell to the shelf above the laundry machines. He took down a folding barber's razor and opened it. "Have you ever seen one of these before? This was how men shaved when I was growing up. None of these silly fifteen blade razors with plastic handles and ridiculous names. Just cold steel."

Mitchell nodded, wiping his eyes. He didn't understand what the razor had to do with anything.

"This is for you," Tony said, still smiling. He took Mitchell's hair in his fist and pulled the boy's head back. With his other hand he slid the blade of the razor into Mitchell's windpipe. It was perfectly quiet, at first. Mitchell didn't struggle or try to make a sound. He just looked at Tony with those wide eyes still red from crying, while blood drooled down from the slit across his throat. And then, a quiet gurgling.

Tony pushed the blade in deeper, holding the boy tightly in case he did start to struggle. Then he reached up for one of the darker towels and wiped the blade clean.

The body in his arms stopped twitching. Tony wrapped the towel around the neck and head, then folded his razor closed. It wasn't Mitchell anymore. Mitchell was gone. He folded the boy up and put him into one of the big laundry bags. He pulled the drawstring tight and slung the bag over his shoulder. In the hallway he smiled at one of the girl campers and tipped his head at her politely.

7.

"There's something not quite Christian about it," Tony said. He sat back in his chair and looked up to where his Bible sat on the shelf. "I can't put my finger on why exactly, but it doesn't seem right for a couple of young ladies to be out there in the middle of the night, obsessing over their telescopes."

Melissa didn't say anything, but she squeezed Joan's hand a bit. The two of them watched Courtney nervously. Courtney didn't like that word, obsessing. They could see her back straighten a bit and that was a bad sign. Cindy, their cabin's counsellor, nodded in agreement with Tony and patted Courtney's shoulder.

"Besides," Cindy said, "if we let you girls do this after lights out, then everyone would want special treatment. I told them no already," she said to Tony, "but they insisted on asking you." She turned back to the girls. "I told you Tony would say the same thing. This is camping! We're supposed to leave all our gadgets behind. No cell phones or video games! Just good times with friends out in the woods."

"This comet has been brightening," Courtney said, "and soon it might even be visible to the naked eye. It's so perfect out here in the middle of nowhere. There's no ambient light. These are really good conditions for observation. And we can't watch it because of a rule that doesn't even make sense." She realized how loud her voice had gotten and tried to bring herself under control. "Even just an hour. Just one hour a night would be enough."

"God made comets," Joan said quietly. "He made stars and galaxies and he made comets. And he made them beautiful. Why would he have made them so beautiful if he didn't want us to enjoy them?"

"You aren't wrong," Tony said to Joan after a moment. "That's very well put. Very well put. What was your name again?"

"Joan," she said.

"I wish I could say yes, Joan," Tony said, "and you do make a very good point. But there are practical considerations here, too. We don't have enough counsellors to spare. We need Cindy to stay with the campers in her cabin, and we can't very well have you three girls out wandering the night by yourselves. It's important that we know where everyone is at all times." He smiled. "We have a responsibility to your parents, after all."

* * *

Margaret turned ten years old just three weeks ago, but she looked older. She was tall and skinny. She looked almost twelve. Her mother lied to get Margaret into the older kid camp. The under ten camp ran later in the summer. It was just better timing. This way her mother and father could align their vacations. They could get away together for the first time in years.

Margaret was used to her cell phone. She never had to remember anyone's number, because their names and numbers were right there, programmed into the small blue phone. It was easy. But there were no cell phones allowed at camp. So her mother had written down her number for Margaret in the front of a little notebook.

"You can call me whenever you like," she said. And then she had driven away.

Like her mother, Margaret had dark, straight hair that constantly fell over her eyes. As she walked across the campground with the notebook clutched in her hand, she was glad to have the hair over her eyes. She was trying not to cry. She knew what was going on. Her mother had told her about menstruation. That's all this was. She was having her first period. It was early but she knew that it was fine and she knew how she was supposed to deal with it. Seeing the blood had been a shock, though. She just wanted to hear her mother's voice. She just wanted to hear her mother say that everything was okay, even if it was just on the phone.

* * *

Martin's mother sent him an email with a picture of the cat with its eyeball dangling out. She had captioned it: "Eye miss you, Martin." In the email she told him she was having fun, and Martin wrote back to tell her about Melissa and Courtney and Joan, and to let her know that things were going good.

"Today we went swimming in the ocean," Martin wrote. "And the salt water tastes so strange. I told Courtney about your tattoo. The beach was covered with huge hopping insects, which Joan said were sand fleas." Martin's mother hated insects. "And I swam! I could even float on my back, which I could never do. Maybe it was only because salt water was more buoyant, but it didn't matter! I swam! I have friends and the summer is going to be good. Eye miss you too."

* * *

37

Mitchell's brother was named John Dee Hemsworth. Sometimes their father called him John, or JD, but he preferred to be called by both first names. He wore all black, usually. It made things easier. Everything went with everything else. And it was harder to get the clothes dirty.

And, to be honest, it had a slimming effect. Not a lot, but every bit helped.

Mitchell still wasn't back and the boredom was getting intolerable. He had even begun flipping through the small red New Testament that his grandmother had given him. But enough was enough. John Dee went into the other room and found Chip writing something in his log book.

"Why hasn't Mitchell come back yet?" John Dee said. "It's been hours now. I thought you said that he was going to talk to Tony." He had heard his brother crying that morning, even before Chip had, but he had done nothing. He'd kept his eyes closed and just tried to ignore him. Mitchell was always crying about something. He was the "sensitive one" their father told people. He was a pussy, was what he was. But pussy or not, it sucked being stuck in this cabin by himself.

"I don't know," Chip said. He looked at his watch. "You want to run over to the main building and see if you can find him? You know where Tony's office is, right? It's on the top floor, at the end of the hall. See if you can get our evening schedule, too, while you're over there."

John Dee jumped down the few wooden steps from the front door of the cabin to the dirt path. Ricky was out there, standing by himself and staring at three girls and that quiet kid Martin, who were all over by the Flying Fox. When John Dee got closer, Ricky spun on him, startled.

"What're you looking at?" Ricky said.

John Dee said nothing, and Ricky pulled his fist back quickly like he was going to punch, then laughed when John Dee flinched. What a charmer. John Dee kept walking. The girls and Martin were taking turns sliding down the wire. They made it look fun. Mitchell had tried to convince him to try it yesterday. Maybe he'd been too quick to laugh it off as a stupid kid's toy.

In the main building, John Dee went past the kitchen and the showers and the laundry room and climbed the curving wooden steps up to the second floor. There was nobody around up here and it was dim inside the building. The shades were pulled on the windows upstairs and all of the doors were closed along the hallway. He could hear the other campers laughing and having fun outside. Meanwhile John Dee was stuck here looking for his pussy older brother.

He knocked on the door to Tony's office. No answer. He knocked again, louder, and there was a muffled sound from inside. Had someone said, "Come in?" John Dee tried the doorknob and it was unlocked. He pushed the door open and went inside.

"Tony?" he said. "Mitchell?" The office was brighter than the hallway. The windows here were open and the sun shone in. But the room was empty. John Dee stood in the doorway with his hand still on the knob, then sighed. Why was everything so difficult with Mitchell?

He stepped back out into the hallway, pulling the door closed behind him.

In the office, Tony kept his hand clamped over Margaret's mouth. Her eyes were wild. She tried to twist out from under him, but she wasn't strong enough. He had her on her back behind the couch, with his knee pressed into her chest. Her shirt lay torn on the floor next to them, split from neck to waist where Tony had cut with the razor. The notebook with her mother's telephone number lay beside the torn shirt.

"Shhh," Tony whispered, holding the razor to his lips like a single finger. "It's okay." Then he reached down and pushed her hair off her face. "Shhh," he said again. They stayed like that, listening to John Dee creak his way back down the hallway, and then he smiled. "Okay," he said. He pushed his knee into her chest harder, shifting his weight until he felt her sternum break with a soft pop. His knee sank a bit deeper into her. Then he took his hand off her mouth and she drew a long, shallow breath, trying to fill her lungs. "Breathe," Tony said. He smiled encouragingly. She was reaching out for her notebook. "That's it," he said. "You're doing good. Breathe."

8.

The sky was still orange and bright, but soon it would be dark enough. Joan set her telescope up on the edge of the playing field and knelt down to examine the dials. Melissa and Courtney had gone to find Cindy, to argue with her again about letting them out late, but Joan knew better than to get her hopes up. There was no sense arguing with adults. No, Joan had decided to make the best of things. Eventually Melissa and Courtney would realize they weren't getting anywhere, that they weren't going to get anywhere, either, and then they'd be out here with her.

"Help me," a voice said behind her. "Please you have to help me." Joan turned to see Ricky stumbling toward her with mud streaked on his cheek. "I think there's a dead body in the woods," Ricky said. "I think there's a dead body in the woods. You have to help me." And he turned back to the woods before Joan could say anything.

"Wait," she called, but Ricky was running back toward the tree line. The camp was the other way. Was he retarded? If there was a dead body, they should go for help. They should find a phone. She took a few steps after him and stopped. "Wait, Ricky!" she yelled. But he kept running, and was halfway to the trees now. If she went after him, she was every bit as stupid as Ricky. She looked down the hill toward where the road to the camp disappeared into the trees. If she didn't stop him, though, he could be in danger. She started running after Ricky as fast as she could.

He was not a very good runner, but he had a head start. Joan ran hard, she was catching up, but he hit the tree line before she caught him. He went crashing into the brush. Joan pulled up short, stopping before she got to the ditch that ran along the tree line. She tried to catch her breath.

"Come on," she called. "We'll go get help and then come back. It'll be safer that way." There was no answer, not at first, but then the bushes shook a little. She could see Ricky now, standing with his back to her, looking down at something. He wasn't very far into the trees.

"It's okay, Joan," Ricky said, and his voice didn't sound scared anymore. She took a step down into the ditch, then stopped. She couldn't see anyone else. So she climbed up into the bushes and pushed through until she was standing beside Ricky. There was no body on the ground. There was nothing here.

Ricky pushed Joan up against the tree and squeezed her shoulder with one hand. He kissed her face hard, his lips closed but his eyes open. She could feel the mud on his face against hers. With his other hand he grabbed at her chest, squeezing blindly. He pinched her skin through the shirt and then tried to grab between her legs. Joan twisted away and kicked him in the shin. She shoved him backward. Ricky stumbled back into the bushes and fell.

Joan ran.

* * *

42

John Dee found Tony standing in front of the tuck shop. Mitchell wasn't with him, though. The head counsellor was laughing and talking with the woman who sold the chocolate bars and candy and drinks. His brown uniform was crisp and ironed. John Dee stood quietly, waiting for them to finish rather than interrupting them.

"Can I help you?" the tuck shop woman said, but John Dee shook his head and looked at the head counsellor.

"Have you seen my brother Mitchell?" he said, and Tony patted his hand on the tuck shop counter as a goodbye to the woman. The he motioned for John Dee to follow and headed up toward the cabins.

"I have indeed seen Mitchell," he said. "You're John? I just sent someone looking for you. Your brother's up at the main building. He's been there since this morning. I tried to calm him down, but there's only so much I can do. I don't think that camp life agrees with him. Fair enough, I suppose," Tony put his hand on John Dee's shoulder. "Not everyone is cut out for the out-doors, John. Personally, I think modern life has made people too delicate. We don't get out and appreciate God's work as often as we should any more. Look at how beautiful this is." He gestured at the trees and the flowers and the sun and wind. At nature. "God's handiwork, John, and we view it as a nuisance."

"He's at the main building?" John Dee said. "I was just up there, I didn't see him."

"I let him use the phone in the janitor's office, in the basement," Tony said. "He was upset. I thought maybe it would be embarrassing for him if the other campers saw him crying. I think he stayed down there to wait for your father."

"Oh," John Dee nodded. Of course he'd called their father. Fucking Mitchell. "So he's going home?" He was going to be stuck here by himself now, while Mitchell went home to video games and air conditioning and internet.

"You both are," Tony said. "Your father thought it would be best. Do you think you could fetch your bags, and Mitchell's, from your cabin, and bring them up to the main building? It's getting dark," He smiled. "Your dad'll be here soon. I'll meet you up there."

* * *

Martin waited while Melissa and Joan argued behind their cabin, Melissa insisting they had to tell their counsellor, Cindy, about Ricky grabbing Joan. Joan didn't want to tell. They went back and forth, first about what would happen to Ricky, and then about whether he was just an idiot or if he was dangerous. Martin didn't say anything. He listened and waited to see if there was anything he could do to help. In the end they asked Martin to tell Ricky to stay the fuck away from them.

"Tell him I will stab him in the face if he even comes near us again," Melissa said.

"I appreciate it, Martin," Joan said. She turned to Courtney. "Will you come with me to get my telescope?"

"Of course," Courtney said. "What time is it? We have chapel soon, don't we?"

"I just don't want to argue any more," Joan said. This conversation was more than Martin had heard Joan say the whole time he had known her.

Martin found Ricky sitting under the Flying Fox, drawing something in the dirt. He looked like he had been crying. Martin didn't want to be angry. He wanted to be calm so that he could talk to Ricky. So he could explain why Ricky was wrong. Being angry got in the way of talking. But Ricky only had one response to Martin's attempt to reason with him.

"What are you, a faggot?" Ricky said. He got up and shoved Martin hard. "You don't like girls, faggot? You don't think I should like girls, faggot?" He shoved Martin again, and Martin stumbled backward. "Faggot," Ricky said, and that was the end of the discussion.

44

9.

John Dee set his suitcases beside Mitchell's on the side steps of the main building. The parking lot was empty and the woods around the camp were dark. He wasn't angry about going home anymore. At least at home, he would be able to watch TV. There were no mosquitoes in the city, either. And all his friends were there. Maybe Mitchell had done them both a favour.

He kicked Mitchell's suitcase and looked around for his brother. Where was he? Was he still down in the basement crying? What a fucking sissy. It had been all day. Even Mitchell couldn't cry this long, could he? Maybe there was a TV down there.

There was a sound from inside, like a chair being knocked over. John Dee looked up the steps at the screen door. Inside there was just darkness. Everyone else was down at the beach for a bonfire. He could hear them off in the distance. The only people in the building should be Mitchell and maybe Tony.

"Mitchell?" he called.

"Yes, it's me," a voice said from the darkness. It wasn't Mitchell's voice. It was high-pitched and too musical. It sounded like an adult pretending to be a child.

"What?" John Dee said. "Mitchell are you there?"

"Yes, it's me, Mitchell," the weird high-pitched voice said from inside. John Dee squinted his eyes, but he couldn't see into the building more than a few feet.

It was definitely a man's voice. Were Mitchell and Tony messing with him? This was too much. It was bad enough he had to sit out here with the suitcases all by himself. It was bad enough he had to wander this camp all day like an idiot, not knowing where his brother was. Before Tony explained things, John Dee had even been worried, at one point. He had been stupidly worried that his brother was hurt or that he'd been pulled out to sea by a strong current. Now his brother and Tony were in there, playing jokes. Making fun of him.

He stormed up the stairs and yanked the screen door open. It was silent inside. The light coming in through the windows only barely lit sections of the large main room.

"I swear to God, Mitchell," John Dee started to say, but then Tony was there, stepping into view, already swinging the heavy sledgehammer through the air with both hands. It struck John Dee in the side of the head, just under his jaw and behind the ear. His head snapped to the side and the sledgehammer crushed bone somewhere in his neck. He staggered. If there was a sound, John Dee didn't hear it.

Tony swung again. The sledgehammer hit him on the same side of the head, this time higher, on the ear. More bone broke, with a far away pulling feeling. John Dee tried to lift his hands to guard his face, but they wouldn't move. Warm blood poured from his ear down his neck and under his shirt collar.

The lights came on in the main room and someone was standing just inside the door behind John Dee. It was one of the girls' counsellors, Jackie. She was holding her nose, with her head tilted back, trying to stop her nosebleed. There was blood on her chin and her hands and down the front of her shirt. She stopped when she saw that she wasn't alone.

It took her a second to figure out that something was wrong with the boy's head. It was bent to the side, like he was trying to understand, but it was bent too far. Then he slumped to his knees, and forward, and Jackie could see the blood on the side of his face. Did he have a nosebleed, too? But then she looked at Tony, smiling at her, friendly as always, a bloody sledgehammer in his hands.

"Oh thank goodness you're here," he said. "I think this poor boy killed himself with a sledgehammer."

* * *

"Didn't there used to be more kids in your cabin?" Courtney said, gesturing with her roasted marshmallow on a stick to where Chip was trying to stop Ricky from whipping Adrian with his marshmallow stick. The only other kids here from the cabin were Gavin and William. Four kids. Five, counting Martin, out of ten.

"I think a couple of them went home today," Martin said. He had seen John Dee packing his suitcase earlier. Martin had gone back to the cabin to make certain that his bed was made. "John Dee and Mitchell went home, for sure," Martin said.

"Or DID THEY?" Melissa said in a spooky voice, holding the flashlight under her face.

* * *

Jackie struggled to get free, but she was tied to a chair. This was the basement of the main building, maybe. It was hard to know for sure. She'd never been down here and she was having a hard time thinking. Tony had dragged her down a flight of stairs. She knew that much.

The sledgehammer had broken her bottom front teeth. Some still had the roots, and those were jagged in her mouth, but some of the teeth were just gone. There was a wet kind of suction in the holes. It should hurt, shouldn't it? But it didn't feel like anything. Just that weird wet suction. She was in shock. She spat some blood on the floor.

Tony came into the room, dragging a body. It was too small to be an adult. Then Jackie remembered the boy. She had caught Tony killing a little boy. She struggled harder. He had crushed the kid's head with a sledgehammer. Why? Why a little boy? Why was this happening? She could see other bodies now, pushed to the sides of the room against the wall. More dead kids? There were four bodies. No, five. Six, counting John Dee.

"I'm sorry to keep you waiting," Tony said. "But I couldn't leave that mess for someone else to clean up. That wouldn't really be fair."

"I, I," Jackie said.

Tony reached up and took an axe off its hook on the wall. Then he turned back to the boy's body, lifted the axe up, and brought it down hard. Jackie wanted to look away, but she couldn't. He was chopping into the shoulder, pulling on the arm with his other hand, trying to separate it like a chicken drumstick. It took some work, but he finally got the arm off. It bent awkwardly at the elbow.

"Why?" Jackie said. "Why are you doing this?"

"I just always wanted to try it," Tony said, standing up with the severed limb. He held it by the forearm, just above the small hand. "It probably won't work," he said, coming toward where Jackie was tied to the chair. He gripped the forearm with both hands like a baseball bat, and swung it so that the shoulder smashed Jackie in the face, mixing John Dee's blood with her own. The blood got in her eyes, but she couldn't wipe it out.

But John Dee's shoulder didn't do very much actual damage. It bloodied her face, it made a mess, and it gave a nice wet thunk every time Tony hit her, but it was not going to be enough.

"I was right," he said. "It didn't work." He sighed and dropped the arm on the floor.

He wiped his hands on his pants, then he took the razor from his back pocket and folded it open. He cut Jackie's throat as deeply as he could. He pushed the razor into her throat harder and harder, using her shoulder for leverage, until the blade scraped on bone.

10.

Cindy turned the shower knob toward the red just a bit more. It was sensitive. Even the slightest movement could turn the water from tepid to scalding in an instant, but she needed the water hot. It helped her calm down. The intensity of the heat on her skin cleared her mind.

She stood there, with her head against the shower wall, letting the scalding water turn her skin pink. She did not notice Ricky peering around the corner from the doorway. He could only see her from behind. Her blonde hair was dark with water.

Cindy sighed. The heat was working. She was calmer. After this, she could go back to her cabin and smile and laugh with the girls and she would try her best not to think about Chip and the things she would do to him later that night. She turned so that her back was against the wall tiles and she ran her hand down her stomach, and on down between her legs. She had small breasts and her nipples were at attention as she touched herself. Ricky drew his breath in sharply. He covered his mouth, but it was too late. Cindy was looking right at him.

Cindy saw Ricky watching, but she kept right on fingering herself. Let the little pervert watch. What did she care? Hell, maybe she should give him a show. She closed her eyes and tilted her head back, opening her mouth and letting herself moan a bit more than she normally would. She used three fingers lightly, pushing and moving in a circle. Slow, then fast. She pulled at her nipple with her free hand.

It was too much. Ricky turned and ran. He stumbled out the front door and down the steps and right into Tony. The head counsellor looked puzzled at Ricky's presence.

"I was," Ricky said, backing away toward the cabins. "I was just going back to my cabin," he said. He had gone into the wrong washrooms by mistake. That was all. Tony smiled and nodded. Ricky smiled back, then turned and ran toward his cabin, relieved to have gotten away with it. He hadn't even noticed the axe in Tony's hands.

Inside, under the hot jets of water, Cindy was getting more worked up. She let out another moan, even louder than before, then she heard a sound halfway across the room. Probably Ricky coming closer, trying to get a better look. Maybe building up the courage to try and touch her.

"Don't push your luck, kid," Cindy said. But she kept her eyes closed and did not stop touching herself. Being watched made her feel dirty. She was close to coming. So close.

With her eyes closed, she didn't see Tony. He lifted the axe into the air, and then brought it down hard with both hands into the crook between her neck and shoulder. She thought the bright pain was an orgasm at first, but it was too bright and there was too much of an edge to it.

The axe cut deep and her feet slipped out from under her. She fell onto her ass. She opened her eyes, and looked up to watch as Tony put his foot against her chest, and tried to yank the axe out of the bone. It was stuck. Tony pushed his foot harder, working the axe up and down a bit while Cindy watched him. It finally came free and she felt that empty faraway sleepiness that she felt after she came. She could just curl up here on the tiles and sleep. She closed her eyes and laid her head on the tile floor, which felt soft and warm. Tony struck her again. Cindy didn't notice.

The shower washed away the blood as it spilled out of her, running across her cheek and away down the drain. Tony turned the shower off, then knelt beside her. He ran his fingers through her hair.

"I would probably look good as a blonde," he said. "Don't you think?" She didn't answer him, but there was a mirror on the far wall. He could see for himself. Tony pulled his razor out, then he started to carefully remove her scalp.

* * *

Ricky came running into the cabin, the screen door banging. He stopped when he saw Martin sitting and folding clothes. Martin didn't look up. It was better if he ignored Ricky and Ricky ignored him. He wanted someone to hurt Ricky. He wanted Melissa and Courtney to beat the hell out of him. He deserved it for trying to hurt Joan. But there was nothing Martin could do himself. So it was better if they ignored each other.

Ricky turned and went into the other room. Martin listened to him stop, then come back to the front door.

"Where's Adrian?" Ricky said, "Or Gavin?"

"Still down at the beach, maybe." Martin said. "How should I know?" He still didn't look at the other boy. There were always flies in the window, beating themselves against the glass. Martin watched them and waited for Ricky to leave. Or threaten him again.

"Well, where's Chip?" Ricky said.

"He's gone to the showers," Martin told him. Ricky turned and walked out without another word. Good riddance. Martin liked it here in the cabin by himself. It was quiet and cool with no one around. There was a cool breeze on his legs. There never seemed to be a breeze when the other campers were here. It was always loud and suffocating.

Martin set his clothes for the next day on top of his suitcase, neatly folded. He still had half an hour before the computer room was off-limits in the main house. Tonight he would send his mother another email. Just something she would see when she woke up, to remind her that he loved her. A picture of him making a face or vomiting tomato juice fake blood with a bed sheet noose around his neck.

"Hey," a voice called from outside. "Hey, Martin." The door was still open, screen and all. Outside, Melissa and Courtney and Joan each had a telescope in their arms. It was Joan who had spoken. "Do you want to see a comet?" Joan said.

"I thought we weren't allowed?" Martin said.

"Cindy's busy off making out with Chip," Melissa said. "And we're supposed to just sit on our beds and wait? Fuck that."

"So are you in?" Courtney said.

"Yes," Martin said. "Yes, I am."

* * *

Chip turned the shower up hotter. He liked it hot. It made him grimace and grimacing made him feel like the star of an old Western. When the water was too hot, it was something to endure. A challenge. He stood in the water, not washing himself or anything, just enduring the heat and grimacing. It was nice to have this time to himself without those fucking children around. Eventually he reached out and turned the water down to a more reasonable temperature so that he could wash. The warm water felt cool by comparison.

He stood facing the wall, rubbing the soap through his chest hair, then up and down each of his arms. He soaped the muscles on his upper arms and his shoulders. While he washed, he thought about soaping up Cindy's body, running the bar over

54

her breasts, circling her nipples. He imagined the suds on her body while her boyfriend stood watching them. Chip felt himself getting hard, and reached down to stroke his penis.

He didn't notice Ricky, peeking around the corner into the shower, watching as Chip stroked himself. Chip put his free arm against the wall for support. He pictured Cindy on her knees in front of him, while her boyfriend watched, powerless to stop them, getting angry but also a bit turned on. After a while, Cindy's boyfriend was stroking an erection through his pants while his girl sucked off another man.

The water was still a bit too hot. Chip grabbed the shower knob, making it cooler on his skin. The boyfriend thing wasn't sexy enough. He needed something else. Chip turned and leaned back against the wall while he jerked off, imagining Cindy in a short skirt with no panties on underneath. She was climbing a ladder, just high enough that he could almost see her pussy. Then she stopped and came back down. She climbed up again, slower this time, a gentle breeze swishing the material of her skirt, promising him a view. But it never moved the material quite far enough.

He heard a small gasp and opened his eyes, startled back to reality. Ricky was watching him, peeking from the doorway. Chip stared at him for a second. Whatever. That was fine, Chip thought, let the little pervert watch. He closed his eyes and leaned back against the wall. He pictured Cindy on the ladder again, this time holding a metre stick, like his elementary school teacher Mrs. North. Chip reached his other hand down to cup his balls. He pictured Cindy climbing up that ladder again. Oh, what a slut, he thought. Climb up. Higher. Higher. But never high enough.

Then one of the bathroom stalls kicked open from inside, the metal door slamming open with a clang. It was Tony. It looked like Tony, anyway. He was wearing a counsellor's uniform and what looked like a wet blonde wig, strands of hair clinging to his forehead.

"Hi, Chip," Tony said in a high-pitched falsetto. "It's me, Cindy," he said and drew the axe out from behind his back. Chip let go of his dick and raised his arms to cover his face. The axe went low, though, chopping into Chip's knee from the side. He staggered, but stayed upright.

"Oh," Chip said. He looked down at gash where the axe had struck him. He let his hands fall to his sides. Tony struck his knee again, the axe cutting further this time. This wasn't right, Chip thought. He looked around for where he had left his underwear. This wasn't supposed to happen with no clothes on. He put his hands over his dick, protecting himself as Tony pulled back for another blow. This time the axe made it most of the way through his knee. The join was split and the kneecap hung from the bottom part of his leg.

Ricky watched in horror from the doorway. Chip fell to the side and didn't lift his hands to cushion his fall. He looked like a tree falling over in the forest, tearing free of its stump.

"Why?" Chip said. He was on his side now, looking up at Tony. "Why are you doing this?" His voice was weirdly calm. He sounded like he was asking an everyday question. What time is chapel tonight? Where did you get that watch? "Why are you doing this?" he said again.

"It's not me," Tony said, kneeling down beside him. Blood was pooling around Tony's sneakers. Chip looked confused and pale. He was still covering himself. "It's you, Chip," Tony said. "You still don't understand, do you?" Chip's head was lolling a bit. "It's been you all along! You went crazy and killed Cindy. You killed those children."

"No," Chip said. He couldn't think properly. "I didn't kill, I didn't kill anyone, did I?" Tony poked him in the bloody knee with the axe. The lower half of Chip's leg was barely attached any more, connected with some tendons. Chip screamed and Tony jumped to his feet with a laugh.

"I'm just kidding, Chip!" Tony said. "It was me!" And with that he stepped back and tilted his head at the naked man.

Then he practice swung the axe, like a golf club, lining up his shot before his real swing, up into Chip's face.

"Gah!" Ricky said, and then clamped his hand over his mouth. Tony looked over at him, and gave a small wave.

"Hi!" he said.

* * *

"Gaaaaaah!" Ricky burst out of the shower building, running toward where Adrian and Gavin were standing. The two were at the base of the Flying Fox zip line, waiting for William to come swinging down so they could have their turns. They heard Ricky but had no idea what the sound was, at first. It was Adrian who spotted him, running their way. Tony was right behind him, axe in hand.

"Gaaaaaaaaaaaaaah!" Ricky said as he passed Adrian. He should tell them to run. But all he could think about was getting away. Into the woods. To the highway. How far was the highway? He kept running. They would run. They would see Tony and the axe and they would run. The woods were right there. And the highway couldn't be that far, could it? Up to the road where the driveway broke off, and then down that road for how long? Oh God, how long had that dirt road been?

"What?" Adrian said, turning to watch Ricky run. "Ha ha, where's the fire?" Adrian said, and then Tony was on him, bashing him in the back of the skull with the blunt side of the axe head, knocking Adrian facedown.

"What the fuck!" Gavin said. William was sliding toward them on the zip line now, lifting his feet and whooping. Tony brought the axe down on the back of Adrian's neck, again and again, right where the spine met the head. He still had Cindy's scalp on his head like a wig, it was slipping off with each swing of the axe. He swung so hard that Cindy's scalp fell off his head, onto his shoulder, landing with the clammy inside of her skin facing up.

57

William landed beside them and stopped laughing when he saw Adrian on the ground. Tony hacked at Adrian's body until he broke through the spine, and the dirt clung to the bloody axe blade like sand on wet bare feet. The body and head were separated.

Tony kicked the head. It rolled!

Gavin took off running after Ricky, but William just stood there, his mouth agape. Tony smiled at him and tried to catch his breath, leaning on the axe handle. He held his hands out to William, to show that he meant no harm. William looked at Adrian's head in the dirt, the eyes open, the face smudged, and thought about his dog, Jeffy. Jeffy's eyes had looked just like that when William had found him lying there in the snow. Tony walked over and patted William on the shoulder. The axe was gone.

"I am out of shape!" Tony said. "Hoo, boy!"

"I," William said, but he never got to finish his sentence. Tony grabbed him by the back of his head, and flicked a straight razor open. He pushed William against the wooden post of the Flying Fox and held him by the jaw. William tried to struggle free, but Tony was already pushing the blade into his throat, and there wasn't much struggle left in him after that.

"Ready or not," Tony yelled in the direction of the two fleeing boys, "here I come!" He wiped his blade on William's face to clean it and dropped the body in the dirt.

11.

Joan had her arm around Martin's. When did that happen? On the walk down through the woods, because he had carried her telescope? Or when they had found the bodies? Martin wasn't sure. She squeezed him closer.

"We have to call for help," Melissa said. Courtney was staring at William's corpse. Tears streamed down her face. There were two dead bodies right there in the middle of the camp ground, Adrian and William, and William's eyes were looking right at her. It felt like his eyes were looking right at her.

Melissa wasn't looking at the body at all. It wouldn't do anybody any good to get upset now. She took Courtney by the shoulder.

"Courtney," Melissa said. "There's a phone in the main building. We can call 911."

"Wait," Courtney said. "Wait. Maybe it's a trick!" There was desperation in her voice. "How do we know it isn't a trick?" She nudged William with her foot, but his eyes just stared blankly. "Maybe they aren't really dead."

She couldn't say the words without glancing over to where Adrian's head sat, detached from his trunk.

"There are two dead kids," Melissa said. "We have to call 911."

Martin reached out his own foot to nudge William's shoulder. He didn't know William, but he could feel fear welling up inside himself. He must have had a family somewhere. He wasn't just a dead body in the dirt. He must have responsibilities.

"What is his mother going to do?" Martin said.

"What?" Melissa said.

"She's going to be all alone now," Martin said. Melissa turned to look at Martin like he'd lost his mind, but before she could say anything, they heard laughter coming from off in the woods. And then a man singing.

"The itsy bitsy spider went up the waterspout," he sang. "Down came the rain and washed the spider out." There was a long pause, then, "Something something something, washed the spider out." It was Tony.

"Please," Ricky cried, off in the darkness. "Please don't hurt me."

And then Ricky was screaming. It echoed all around them, screams getting higher- and higher-pitched, until they weren't recognizable anymore. He kept screaming after that, too, until eventually the voice wasn't even recognizable as human. It was like when you wrote a word over and over again until it looked alien and wrong.

* * *

Joan looked down at the dead bodies on the ground and then out at the woods, where Ricky was still screaming. Okay. This wasn't difficult to figure out. This was simple.

"Tony is killing people," Joan said. "He has gone crazy and he is murdering people. Melissa's right. We have to call for help. We have to get out of here."

"We don't know that," Courtney said. "It could just be a big prank." She was still crying. She was going to be murdered, Martin thought. The one who loses control always gets murdered. She'll run off or just fall to her knees crying at exactly the wrong time, and she won't make it out alive.

"I hope I'm wrong," Joan said. "But we have to act like I am right. If I'm wrong, it's no big deal. Nobody will blame us for calling the police. But if I'm right, and we waste time trying to figure out if it's a trick or not, it'll just give him more time to get us."

"Where are all the other kids?" Martin said. All of the cabins around them were dark. The boys' cabins sat back in the woods a bit, completely in shadow, and there were no lights from the girls' cabins up on the ridge.

"First, 911," Melissa said. She grabbed Courtney's arm. Courtney kept looking at William, but took a couple stumbling steps sideways as Melissa pulled her. Finally she turned and the four of them ran for the main building.

"There's a phone at the back," Melissa told Joan. "You and Martin go back there. Call 911, and tell them where we are. Tell them what happened."

"We don't know what happened," Courtney said. The screaming outside had stopped and Martin was suddenly aware of how brightly lit they were in the hallway. They couldn't see out at all. But anyone out there could see them.

Splitting up was very clearly a bad idea. They shouldn't split up. It didn't make any sense. They would split up and Tony would come back quietly and find them, one by one.

"We can't split up," Martin said, still holding tight to Joan.

"There's a phone at the back by the kitchen," Melissa said, "and the confiscated cell phones are up in Tony's office. We'll split into teams. Think of it logically, Martin. That gives us two chances. Even if the phone lines are cut, then the team with the cell phone can still call 911. And if the team with the cell phone gets caught, the others can call from downstairs. There's no way he can stop us both fast enough."

"What if the phone lines are cut, and he stops the cell phone team first?" Joan said. Melissa gave her a dirty look.

"Then we're pooched," Melissa said. "What would you rather do, go running into the woods like Ricky? That sounds like it worked out really well for him."

Melissa and Courtney went upstairs and Joan led Martin straight to the kitchen. She found the biggest knife she could, a large chef's knife, and she held it like a weapon. It was heavy and it felt satisfying in her hand. But who was she kidding? What was she going to do with that? Stick it into Tony? Joan pictured herself trying to stab somebody.

"The phone's at the back," Martin said.

"Grab a knife," Joan said. "But keep it hidden. Don't let anyone see it until it's too late. When you take it out, you have to use it fast and as hard as you can. My father told me," she said, "that most of the time, people try to scare somebody with a knife, and end up getting their knife taken away and used on them. The knife is a surprise. You can't give Tony any time to react to it." Martin picked up one of the kitchen knives, too. He made stabbing motions in the air and shook his head.

"This is weird," he said. "This is too weird." Joan took his hand and squeezed it. Her fingers were cold. They stood there in the dark kitchen, holding hands, and the building around them was quiet. They couldn't hear Melissa or Courtney upstairs and there was no sound from outside. Maybe if they stayed just like this, everything would be okay. This felt safe and right, with Joan holding his hand.

But it wasn't safe at all.

In the back office, the phone was ripped right out of the wall. The rest of the office seemed neat and tidy. Was this the last chance? Martin went over to the desk, and started pulling open drawers.

"What're you doing?" Joan said. "We have to go find Melissa."

"I'm looking for a pen," Martin said.

"A pen?" Joan laughed. "Are you going to send a letter to the police?"

12.

Just before the top of the stairs, Courtney stopped. Adrian's head sat on the top step staring at them. Blood dribbled down from the neck and onto the next step down. The head had been waiting for them, Courtney was certain. It had just been sitting here on the top step waiting patiently for them.

"Oh God," Courtney said. "Oh God, I can't."

"It can't hurt you," Melissa said, pulling her by the arm. "Don't do this, Courtney. We have to get those cell phones. We don't have time to stand around crying. Come on." But Courtney wouldn't move. Melissa let go of her and shrugged. "Fine, you wait here and cry, then. Guard the head. I am going to go and save everybody while you finish crying."

Melissa walked down the hallway quickly. She was angry and she didn't know why. She should be scared. She should be crying, the way Courtney was, but all she could think were angry thoughts. What had she done to deserve this bullshit? Who did Tony think he was? She had thought he was a creep, right from the beginning. That talk he gave about accepting Jesus into your heart and the little girl being so sad she was going to miss the bonfire. It was so phony. Maybe she hadn't known he was an axe murderer, but she had known he was wrong.

The door to Tony's office was open and the light was on. There was no sound. Melissa peeked into the room. Tony's office phone sat in the middle of the floor with its cut cord wrapped neatly around it. Everything else in the office was in its place, tidy.

The cell phones would be in his desk. She made her way around the couch toward the desk and there on the floor was Margaret's body. She was small and her chest was caved in. There were dark bruises around her throat. Her eyes were closed peacefully, at least.

The floor behind the couch was covered with smashed cell phones. Shards of plastic casing, small circuit boards. Little wires. Behind her, Tony stepped out of the darkness of the hall, with the axe already swinging through the air. Melissa had begun to drop to her knee, to examine one of the smashed cell phones that looked almost whole. Her head dropped, so that her neck was safe from the axe, but it didn't drop far enough. The blade of the axe split her skull.

With the razor blade, Tony tried to cut off Melissa's face. He pushed the blade in behind her ear and he could feel it cutting through muscle and tendons, but it just wouldn't peel away from the bone. He scraped along the bone underneath the eyebrow, and finally the top section of the little girl's face came free.

But it looked fake and plastic, stretched and pulled like this. It didn't look like a scared little girl at all. He gripped the bottom of her jaw with his fingers, and worked her mouth like a puppet.

"Tony," Melissa said in a high-pitched voice. "Tony, I miss my friends!"

"Well, what does that have to do with me?" Tony said.

"Please go murder my friends so we can all be together in the bloody place," Melissa said in Tony's falsetto voice.

He left Melissa on the floor, a small pool of blood under her skull, half of her face drooping where it wasn't properly attached anymore.

* * *

Courtney stood in silence at the top of the stairs. She couldn't see down the hallway to where Tony's office was, but she could hear someone coming toward her. It was Melissa. It had to be Melissa. She had a cell phone and they were going to be okay. They would call 911 and tell the operator that they were at the Bible Camp. Please send some squad cars. Then they would just have to hide until help arrived.

The footsteps were quiet and slow, which made sense. Melissa was being as quiet as she could. Courtney had stopped crying a bit. This would all be over soon. They could go home. The city had too much ambient light, but it would be so nice to set her telescope up on her balcony again. She would set up the chair and put the radio on and she would be okay. Down the hallway, one of the footsteps fell heavier. It was loud and hard, and then another fell. The footsteps were running toward her now. It was Melissa, it had to be Melissa. Courtney closed her eyes and squeezed her fists.

In his rush at the girl on the stairs, Tony's foot kicked Adrian's head, which went rolling and bouncing down the stairs. He lifted the axe above his head again and tried to focus on the girl.

* * *

Joan and Martin were at the top of the stairs to the first landing when Adrian's head rolled down and hit the wall right ahead of them. Joan put her arm out to stop Martin short. Above them, on the stairs, they could hear Courtney whimpering. There was a man's voice, too, but they couldn't make out what he was saying.

Joan held her knife in her fist tightly.

"This is it," she said. "He's at the top of the stairs. We know where he is, and he doesn't know where we are. This is our chance. He can't attack us both at the same time. If he goes after you, I will stab him from behind. If he goes after me, you have to get him, Martin. Can I count on you?"

Martin opened his mouth to answer, but then Tony was there, grabbing Joan by the hair. She lifted the knife but Tony grabbed hold of her wrist, moving his hand to cover hers, so that she still held the knife tightly but he was in control. He used her hand to jab the knife into her cheek, and then again.

"Stop stabbing yourself!" Tony said. He smiled at Martin, and then made Joan stab herself in the face again. "Stop stabbing yourself!" They were small cuts, not deep. But the next jab went into her eye, and Joan let out a scream. When Tony pulled her hand and the knife away, there was no blood. But her eye began to sag out of shape.

Martin tightened his grip on his own knife. He had to help her but he couldn't move. Joan was looking at him with her one good eye, helplessly. She struggled against Tony's controlling hand, but it did no good. He made her lift the knife up again, and this time forced the blade into her mouth. She clamped her teeth shut, but he wedged the tip in between then, prying her mouth open enough to shove the blade in deeper. Joan struggled and Tony let go of her hair, pushing her back against the wall, and he used both hands now, shoving the knife into the back of her throat.

Blood spilled out over her chin and she struggled harder. Tony twisted the knife sharply, then twisted it the other way. He opened his hand and slammed his palm on the butt of the knife handle, driving it into her spine at the back of her throat. Joan stopped struggling. He let her slide to the floor, the knife handle jutting from her mouth. She was perfectly still, except for her left leg. Her left leg kicked a little. Then lay still. Then kicked a little.

Martin dropped his own knife and ran like hell.

13.

Tony went back up to the main building and changed into his regular clothes. He folded his wet, bloodied uniform neatly and set it on the chair by his office window. He swept up the shards of cell phone, except the bits that were in Melissa's blood. The blood had to stay.

"Goodnight, Comet," he said to Margaret's lifeless body, "Goodnight, Cupid," he said to Melissa, and he turned out the office light. Then he went down the hall and stopped beside Courtney's body. "Goodnight, Donner," he whispered to her. He took the stairs two at a time, stopping at the landing between floors, where Joan lay slumped against the wall and Adrian's head sat staring into the corner. "Goodnight Blitzen!" Tony said to Joan. "Goodnight, goodnight! Parting is such sweet sorrow." He stopped beside beside Adrian's head and gave it one last gentle kick. It rolled down the stairs and Tony smiled.

He locked the door behind him as he left. Then he got in his car and drove home to his wife and children, who were asleep. He climbed into bed with his wife and in the morning he made his children breakfast.

It was two days before someone drove out to the camp and found the bodies. And then it took a few more hours after that for them to realize who was missing and then to look up where he lived.

When they came for Tony, they found his wife setting the table for lunch. They were having chicken fingers and french fries. She set out the ketchup and the salt and the pepper. The children were playing in the back yard, shrieking with laughter. Suddenly, men with guns were everywhere, in the kitchen, in the back yard. Then snatching the children up into their arms, smashing in windows, kicking over tables, storming up the stairs, yelling, "Clear!" after every door they kicked in.

"Where is your husband?" one of the policemen demanded.

"Tony?" his wife said, shocked. "He just went to get some milk."

They found Tony at the store, a carton of milk set on the counter in front of him. The police cruisers screeched into the corner store's parking lot, and the clerk looked up. Tony put a five dollar bill on the counter between them.

"Keep the change," Tony said.

Then the police were on him. They shoved him face down on the ground and handcuffed him behind his back, driving a knee into his spine. One of the policemen spit on him. They pulled him to his feet and started reading him his rights, but Tony just kept shaking his head.

"Wait, wait, wait," he said, and everyone stopped to listen. "This is about those children I murdered, isn't it?" He laughed. "God," he said. "When did it become illegal to have a good time?"

* * *

The police spent a whole day photographing the camp. They had a list of the campers and it was very difficult matching names to the bodies they found, or to the parts of the bodies. The counsellors were easier. In Tony's office the police found photocopies of the counsellors' ID cards, along with the background checks.

Eventually they had to ask the parents to provide photographs and then they had to ask the parents to come in to verify the identities in person. Every piece of paper was taken into evidence.

In the main building, there was a downstairs office. In the top drawer of the desk there, the police found a folded note: "To Mom, From Martin." There was a boy named Martin among the dead.

The note read, "Don't worry, I won't leave you alone. If I don't get away, then I promise I will haunt you!"

* * *

Tony pulled Martin by the hair, dragging the boy toward the beach and the sound of waves. The air smelled like salt and the moon looked lovely up above the ocean. Martin fought, but the harder he fought, the more it felt like his hair was being torn out of his head. He grabbed at Tony's hands, and tried to hold on.

The water was ice cold and they didn't go out very deep before Tony stopped and let go of Martin's hair. Tony looked around and let out a sigh.

"Look at this," Tony said. "It's beautiful, isn't it? It makes you glad to be alive, doesn't it? Take a minute, enjoy it."

Martin sat in the water with the waves coming up almost to his shoulders and then rolling past him. Every wave seemed to lift him up, just a little, and carry him back away from Tony, toward land.

"Okay," Tony said, and he took hold of Martin's head again, and forced him down under the water. He put all his weight into it, driving Martin's face into the sand and rocks of the beach. The salt stung inside Martin's nose, but he couldn't struggle with Tony on him. He thought about his mother coming home to an empty apartment and he couldn't help it, he took a deep lungful of water. It felt terrifying. He couldn't stop. He breathed in salt water and the stirred-up sand filled his lungs. Above him, it sounded like Tony was singing something again and he could hear the waves too, sort of, but it was all fading. He thought about his mother's face, smiling, and he held that picture in his mind for the rest of his life.

The End

Acknowledgements

Thank you to Doctor Priyadarshani Raju for her medical expertise regarding the practical aspects of murdering children, and the impracticality of using pieces of murdered children to murder an adult.

Also, thank you to Bryanna Reilly, Tim Maly, Jeff Grantham, Maggie Dort, Emily Horne, Ryan North, my mom, the Malagash Bible Camp, and Mike Saturday Lecky. Hail Satan.

Murder Index

About the Author

Joey Comeau is the author of *Lockpick
Pornography*, *Overqualified*, and *One Bloody
Thing After Another*. He lives in Canada
and, with photographer Emily Horne,
he makes the webcomic A Softer World.
Google that shit.

Made in the USA
Lexington, KY
17 November 2010